Higby

THE AVERAGE MONKEY

TODD AARON SMITH

BARBOUR
PUBLISHING

For Veronica

Visit Higby at
www.higbyonline.com

© 2003 by Todd Aaron Smith

Edited by Phil A. Smouse

ISBN 1-58660-857-6

Published by Barbour Publishing, Inc., P.O. Box 719, Uhrichsville, Ohio 44683 www.barbourbooks.com

 Member of the
Evangelical Christian
Publishers Association

Printed in China.

5 4 3 2 1

Higby the monkey had BIG dreams.
He wanted to be important. He wanted
to make a difference! He wanted to
be more than just an average monkey.

Higby loved his
life in the zoo, but
he wondered what
it might be like to
do other things.

A little girl and her mother stopped to visit Higby in his cage. "That monkey is so cute!" said the little girl. She wanted to stay and give Higby a hug, but her mother was ready to move along. "Good-bye, Higby the cute monkey!" The little girl giggled. *Good-bye.* Higby smiled. Then she blew him a kiss and she skipped away.

Higby liked the little girl. He was sad to see her go. But he was not sad for long. It was time to eat—and Higby loved to eat!

One of the zoo workers brought a big basket of fruit and nuts and other yummy things to Higby's cage just as she had done many times before.

The zoo worker set the basket on the floor. "Time to lock up," she said as she stepped back out of the cage. When she turned her key, the big lock closed with a thump.

But something was wrong—the door was still open! The zoo worker did not notice. The visitors did not notice. The other animals did not notice. No one noticed—no one but Higby!

Higby leaned on
the door—and he tumbled
right out of his cage.

Higby was free! *This is it!* he thought. *Maybe now I can
be important. Maybe now I can make a difference.
Maybe now I can be more than just an average monkey!*

Higby was a little monkey,
but he had some big dreams.
He decided to see what
adventures might be waiting
for him outside the zoo.
He tiptoed around to the
back of his cage and headed
straight for the exit!

"Where do you think you're going?" a long, low voice asked from somewhere way up in the sky.

Higby turned around and saw a giraffe looking down at him. "I'm going to do something important!" the little monkey replied.

"What can *you* do?"
the giraffe snickered.

Higby thought for a moment.
"I'm not really sure,"
he said softly. "But I'll
know when I find it!"

"Oh, Higby." The giraffe
laughed. "You won't find
anything important to do.
You're just an average monkey."

"Besides," the giraffe snorted, "I don't see YOUR picture on *the sign!*"

Higby looked up at the big zoo sign. It showed an elephant, a bear, a tiger, and a giraffe.

"They only put *important* animals on the sign!" sneered the giraffe.

"I guess you're right." Higby sighed. His little heart was broken. He wanted to go back to his cage, but deep down inside Higby knew he was important, too! After a moment, he turned and left the zoo.

Higby went out into the big city. He saw a police officer directing traffic. *Now that looks important!* the little monkey thought. So he jumped right into the middle of the busiest intersection in town. He was going to direct traffic, too!

But Higby didn't
know what to do.

He waved his
big fuzzy
hands.

He stood on
his head.

He spun around and around
and flapped his arms like a bird.
Soon Higby was very dizzy.
The drivers were very dizzy, too!

Higby had made quite a mess. Cars were scattered in every direction. People were honking their horns. "Hey!" shouted the police officer. "What's going on over there?"

I guess monkeys do not make very good police officers, Higby thought as he ducked out of sight.

Higby wandered down
the busy city street.
The beautiful buildings
and huge crowds were
amazing. He saw big buses
and shiny yellow taxis with
people riding inside. And
the buildings were so tall
they seemed to disappear
into the clouds.

Then Higby saw something else. It was a bus—with no one inside! *At last I can make a difference!* he thought.

A bus can take people wherever they need to go. That's a very big job—even for a little monkey!

Higby climbed into the bus. He sat down
behind the big steering wheel. He stomped
the gas pedal all the way down to the floor.
And as the bus roared out into traffic
Higby remembered something very important:
He didn't know how to drive!

BAAM! The bus crashed through a gate and landed in the museum fountain! Higby was lucky that no one was hurt. *I guess monkeys do not make very good bus drivers,* he thought.

Higby snuck back into the city. His pride was a little bumped and bruised. His heart was, too. The little monkey knew he could make a difference. He just wasn't sure what to do. He shuffled past an enormous metal gate. There were thousands of happy people on the other side. *What are all those people cheering about?* he wondered.

The crowd surrounded a beautiful green field
where some big men were playing a game.

Wow! thought Higby. *Those men must be very important.
Look at how everyone loves them—and all they do is play!*

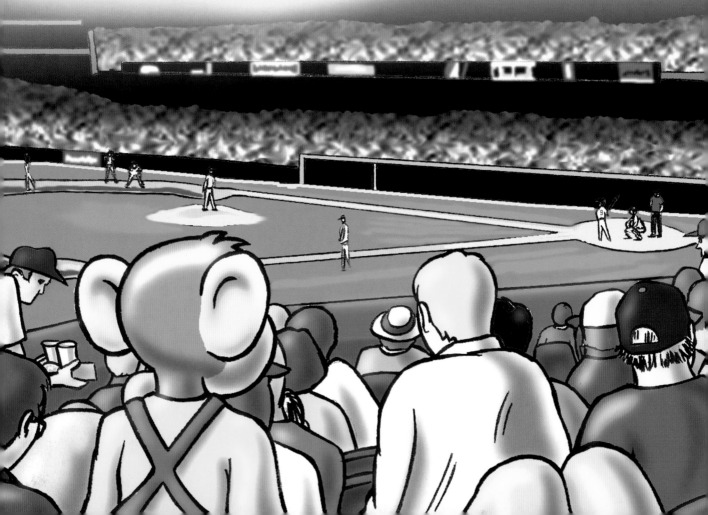

Higby froze in his tracks. *I may not be big or important*, the little monkey thought with a smile. *But I do know how to play! KA-POW!* Higby bolted through the crowd. He jumped down onto the field! He scooped up the ball and started running away just as fast as he could!

The players started shouting. The fans started shouting!
The men chased Higby all the way across the field.
Higby climbed the big green wall and jumped
down on the other side.
The crowd roared with laughter.
They had never seen anything
like this at a ballgame before!

STADIUM EXIT

But the players did not think Higby was funny. He didn't mean to make them mad—but they were mad just the same. *I guess monkeys do not make very good ballplayers*, he thought.

He shuffled out of the park and headed for home.

ZOO STAFF ENTRANCE

**VISITORS PLEASE
USE MAIN GATE** →

Higby returned to the zoo. It was a nice place, but he was very sad. He wanted to be important. He wanted to make a difference, but nothing he did ever seemed to work out. *The giraffe was right,* Higby thought. *I'm just an average monkey.*

It was getting dark. The zoo would be closing soon. Higby went back to his cage and pulled himself up onto his little wooden swing. Then he thought about this very disappointing day. *What's a monkey to do?* Higby sighed.

Just then Higby
heard a tiny
voice. "You are
so cute!" the
voice whispered.
Higby looked up.

It was the little girl!
"Look!" She smiled.
"I have a brand-new stuffed toy—
and it looks just like you!"

Higby saw the toy.
It DID look like him!
"You are my favorite
animal in the whole
zoo!" said the little
girl. "I found this
toy in the gift shop.
I can't wait to take
it to school and
show all of my
friends. I'm going
to tell them all
about you!"

Higby didn't know what to think! He had made the little girl happy. He had made a difference. He had been important the whole time! He didn't need to be a police officer or a bus driver or a famous ballplayer. All he had to do was be *himself!* *Maybe there is no such thing as an average monkey!* Higby thought. *Maybe God really does make each and every person special in his or her own way!*

The zoo became quiet. The animals went to sleep for the night. Higby was very tired, too. As he drifted off to sleep he smiled and thought to himself, *I am more than an average monkey!* Then he thanked God for making him special in his own very special way.

I'm special—
just because I'm Higby.